STO

ALLEN COUNTY PUBLIC LIBRARY

3 1833 03945 9265

P9-ECK-945

Gregory Is Grouchy!

And Other Really Good Reasons to Be COMPASSIONATE

Kirkland street.

WELCOME TOMMY!

Faith KiDs

Written and illustrated by Sandy Silverthorne

Allen County Public Library
900 Webster Street
PO Box 2270
Fort Wayne, IN 46801-2270

Dedication:
To my Eugene family, Nanee, Art, Gerri,
Amy, Daniel, Melody and Nathaniel.
Thanks for adopting me.

FaithKids® is an imprint of Cook Communications Ministries,
Colorado Springs, Colorado 80918
Cook Communications, Paris, Ontario
Kingsway Communications, Eastbourne, England

GREGORY IS GROUCHY!
© 2001 by Sandy Silverthorne for text and illustrations

All rights reserved. Except for brief excerpts for review purposes,
no part of this book may be reproduced or used in any form
without written permission from the publisher.

Designed by Keith Sherrer
Edited by Kathy Davis

First hardcover printing, 2001
Printed in Singapore
05 04 03 02 01   5 4 3 2 1

Library of Congress Cataloging-in-Publication Data

Silverthorne, Sandy, 1951–
        Gregory is grouchy! : and other really good reasons to be compassionate / written
and illustrated by Sandy Silverthorne.
                p. cm. — (Kirkland Street kids)
        Summary: When Gregory is unkind to a new classmate, the teacher assigns a
science fair project on compassion.
        ISBN: 0-7814-3524-2
        [1. Kindness—Fiction. 2. Schools—Fiction. 3. Christian life—Fiction.] I. Title.

PZ7.S5884 Gr 2001
[E]—dc21   00-064625

There was something about the new kid that just made Gregory's skin crawl.

From the minute Tommy walked into Miss Fronebush's room, Gregory knew he was trouble. He had his perfect little button-down shirt and his perfect notebook and his perfect new backpack. He was really smart and funny, and he was also a good tetherball player.

But he talked just a little too loudly and laughed just a little too often.

Gregory was never wrong about who was good and who was bad in his school.

After all, he'd been watching TV since he was little, and he always knew who was good and bad on TV. This new kid was bad news.

Gregory was going to make Tommy's life miserable.

Gregory had been at Kirkland Elementary since kinder-
garten. He knew everybody, and everybody knew him.
That made him feel good. At recess, Gregory told
Bradley, Tyler, Jake, Josh, and the other Josh
to keep away from
Tommy.

Don't talk to him
or you'll become
just like him!

"Yeah, look at him with his perfect little button-down shirt," Bradley said. Bradley obviously got the picture.

Whenever Tommy tried to talk to anyone on the playground, Gregory would yell, "Don't talk to him or you'll become just like him!"

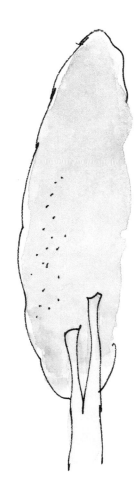

During art the kids were drawing what they wanted to be when they grew up. Gregory was drawing an astronaut; Marpel was drawing a psychologist. Gregory looked at Tommy's paper. He was drawing an airplane.

"That's stupid," Gregory said. "You're too dumb to fly an airplane!"

"My dad's a pilot," Tommy answered. "He'll teach me."

"Oh, sure, Tommy. Right." By now Gregory was laughing so hard he was snorting.

Oops. Miss Fronebush always managed to appear whenever Gregory was doing something wrong. "Are you making fun of Tommy?" she asked.

"That depends," Gregory said. "How much have you heard?"

Wrong answer.

Gregory hated staying in from recess. Especially three days in a row.

Meanwhile, Marpel had a similar problem. You see, Ruth Ann Festerman just didn't get it. Her hair was kind of frizzy and she had big ears. And what was with her outfit? Rumor had it she lived in a cardboard box just outside of town.

Marpel and Ruth Ann had eaten lunch together outside while everyone else was eating in the cafeteria. Ruth Ann seemed nice enough, even if she dressed weird and had no table manners.

But when the other girls showed up and started making fun of Ruth Ann, Marpel had to save herself.

Being seen with Ruth Ann could set her social status back years.

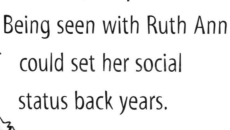

So Marpel shouted, "Ruthy Ann, Ruthy Ann lives in a box and sleeps in a can."

Marpel could get extremely creative when push came to shove.

Ruth Ann just sat there. She didn't feel much like eating anymore.

Back in the classroom, all this non-recess time had given Gregory a chance to think about his science fair project. For some reason Miss Fronebush had decided that Gregory's topic should be compassion. *How can I combine being kind to people with my amazing scientific ability?* Gregory wondered.

That night Gregory asked his dad for help.

"Compassion, huh?" Gregory's dad began. "The way I try to understand others is to spend some time in their shoes."

That sounded gross. "Aren't you afraid of toe fungus?" asked Gregory.

"No, I mean you try to think about what they're feeling. When you can see things from another person's point of view, you can have compassion for him."

Other people's shoes. Hmmmm. This had possibilities.

The next afternoon, Gregory burst through the kitchen door with his newest creation. "What is it?" his mom asked.

"It's my invention for the science fair. I call it the **Compassionometer**."

Gregory's contraption was an old steel helmet attached by wires to a pair of oversized shoes. "This amazing device gives you the ability to put yourself in other people's shoes just by looking at them. Let me show you how it works."

Gregory placed the helmet on his head, adjusted the goggles, and flipped the switch. The contraption made a whirring sound and lit up. The reflection made Gregory's head look all purple.

"It's working!" he shouted as he turned toward his mom. Instead of seeing his mom standing there, Gregory now saw her walking through the house picking up his stuff off the floor. Then he saw her fixing dinner and taking care of the little kids while trying to keep Gregory's room neat.

"Wow, that's amazing," said Gregory. "I guess it's not completely working yet."

The night of the science fair, Gregory sat on a stool
wearing his new creation. On his right, Bradley was
showing how connecting a wire to a battery created
a magnet.

To his left, Sarah had put together an aquarium display.

While most of the people managed to avoid Gregory's exhibit, occasionally someone would stop by for some amusement.

Halfway through the evening, Tommy and his mom walked up. "Hi, Gregory," Tommy said quietly.

Wow, this was Gregory's chance for revenge. He completely forgot he was wearing the Compassionometer as he tried to think of something mean to say to Tommy. Gregory took a deep breath and blurted out, "Hi, Tommy. How's it goin', buddy?"

Buddy? Gregory never called anyone buddy. What was happening? *I know,* thought Gregory, *I'll shove him when nobody's looking.*

When Tommy's mom turned to watch Bradley pick up a nail with his electromagnet, Gregory made his move. But instead of shoving Tommy, Gregory's arm shot out and he patted Tommy on the back. "Good to see you, buddy."

Buddy! **AUGHHHHHH!** He'd said it again! He turned to look at Tommy, and that's when the Compassionometer really kicked in.

What Gregory saw wasn't Tommy the jerk, but Tommy a couple of weeks ago at home. His mom was talking to him and he looked like he was crying. "It's going to be okay," Tommy's mom was saying. "You'll see Dad every other weekend, and you can spend a couple of weeks with him in the summer."

Gregory just stood there silently watching the scene through the Compassionometer.

"But why can't you guys just stay together?"
Tommy cried, covering his face with his hands.

Gregory was stunned. **Divorce?** *Oh, no!* he thought.
Tommy was in a new school because his parents had
split up, and Gregory had
been making his life
miserable.

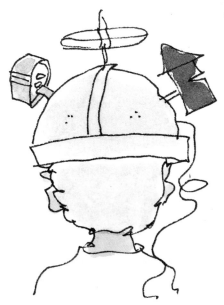

Then another thought hit him. *What if, when I take off the Compassionometer,*

I go back to being mean again?

Gregory stood there feeling sicker by the minute. He had to get out of there.

As he turned to make his escape, he caught his own reflection in Marpel's endless mirror exhibit. He looked funny in the big silver helmet and flashing lights.

But wait. The Compassionometer was working on him!

Suddenly he could see why he didn't like Tommy. There was Tommy surrounded by Gregory's friends. And there was Gregory... **all by himself.** Tommy was getting the attention Gregory had always had. Gregory was jealous!

This Compassionometer was becoming annoying. But it did help Gregory figure out what was making him feel so miserable inside.

Gregory slowly slipped the helmet off his head. He turned around and looked at Tommy.

Whew! The compassionate feeling was still there. Gregory reached out and shook Tommy's hand. "I'm sorry I've been such a jerk to you. I'd really like to be your friend."

Tommy didn't know what to say.

"Do you want to see how this thing works?" Gregory was just about to put the helmet on Tommy's head when Marpel showed up.

"Hold it, buster, it's my turn!" she shouted as she slipped on the headpiece.

As chance would have it, the first person to walk by was Ruth Ann Festerman.

Sure enough, Marpel looked right at her. But instead of seeing dumb old Ruth Ann, she saw her all alone in a run-down house getting ready for school.

Both her parents were at work already. She opened the
refrigerator and there was a stick of butter and two
cans of soda. So once again she left for school hungry.

Marpel felt awful. Ruth Ann's life was hard, and she had
made her feel even worse. *What do I do now?* Marple
wondered.

After the science fair, Gregory, his dad, and Tommy went
to McBanback's for a snack. "Yeah, I'd sure like to be nicer
and put myself in other people's shoes, but wearing this
Compassionometer all the time would get pretty old,"
Gregory said.

His dad laughed. "Actually, we have our own Compassion-ometer built right inside of us. We just have to remember to use it."

Gregory looked confused. His dad continued, **"It's God's Spirit.** Once we know the Lord, He'll help us see people the way He sees them. And He'll even help us to be nice to them."

From then on, things were different at Kirkland Elementary. Gregory and Tommy took the Compassionometer to school and helped all the kids try it on. Once they saw what it felt like to walk in someone else's shoes, most started using their built-in Compassionometers and treating each other much better.

After spending some time in her shoes, Marpel was extra nice to Ruth Ann and defended her if other kids made fun of her. Marpel even gave Ruth Ann some of her clothes that didn't fit anymore.

Of course, Marpel's never been known for her fashion sense ...

Faith Parenting Guide

Gregory Is Grouchy!
And Other Really Good Reasons to Be Compassionate

Ages: 4-7

Life Issue: My child is learning to care about others.

Spiritual Building Block: Compassion

Learning Styles: Help your child learn about God's Word
in the following ways:

 Sight: Review the story together by looking at and talking about the pictures in the book. As you study the illustrations of Tommy and Ruth Ann, look carefully at their expressions and talk about how each child may have felt at different points in the story: hurt, left out, shy, sad, surprised, happy, etc. Help your child understand the meaning of compassion and the importance of seeing things from another's point of view.

 Sound: Ask your child these questions about the story:
•Why did Gregory dislike Tommy? (Gregory was jealous.)
•Why did Marpel stop being friendly to Ruth Ann? (Ruth Ann wasn't popular, and Marpel was afraid of what her friends would think.)
•How does showing compassion change the way we treat others? (Once we know and understand others, we care about them more. We put them ahead of ourselves.)
•What can you do to show compassion for somebody you know at school or in the neighborhood? (Help your child think of concrete acts of caring for others.)

 Touch: Encourage your child to show compassion to others, even strangers, by collecting toys and clothing to donate to the Salvation Army, Goodwill, or other organization. Or help your child participate in local food drives when available. Talk about the items you have chosen and have your child imagine how a needy child might feel about receiving the things you have contributed.